# Dora's World Adventure!

adapted by Suzanne D. Nimm
based on the teleplay written by Valerie Walsh
illustrated by Tom Mangano

Simon Spotlight/Nick Jr.
New York   London   Toronto   Sydney

Based on the TV series *Dora the Explorer*® as seen on Nick Jr.®

SIMON SPOTLIGHT
An imprint of Simon & Schuster Children's Publishing Division
1230 Avenue of the Americas, New York, New York 10020

Manufactured in the United States of America
18 20 19 17
ISBN-13: 978-1-4169-2447-0
ISBN-10: 1-4169-2447-7
0210 LAK

*¡Hola!* I'm Dora! Today is Friendship Day: *¡El Día de la Amistad!* On Friendship Day friends around the world have parties and wear special friendship bracelets. If we wear our bracelets, we'll all be friends forever and ever! Do you want to see the friendship bracelets?

The friendship bracelets are so beautiful!
Oh, no! There's Swiper, and he's trying to swipe our friendship bracelets! Let's stop Swiper from swiping our bracelets. Say "Swiper, no swiping!"

Look! Swiper has been swiping bracelets from all around the world. But he didn't know they were special *friendship* bracelets. There won't be a Friendship Day unless everyone has a friendship bracelet, Swiper! We need to return them!

Swiper and I are going to travel around the world and return the bracelets to all our friends for Friendship Day. Will you come with us? Great!

Who do we ask for help when we don't know which way to go? Yeah, Map!

Map says that to return the friendship bracelets to our friends, we have to go to the Eiffel Tower in France, to Mount Kilimanjaro in Tanzania, to the Winter Palace in Russia, and to the Great Wall of China.

*¡Vámonos!* Let's go around the world!

We're in France! And this is my friend Amelie! To say
"hello" to Amelie in French, we say "bonjour." Let's say
"bonjour" to Amelie. Bonjour, Amelie!
    Amelie is going to help us bring the bracelets back to
the Eiffel Tower.

Amelie says that the smiling gargoyle will help us find the Eiffel Tower. There's the smiling gargoyle! The smiling gargoyle says that we need to follow the street with the diamond stones. Do you see the diamond stones? Great! We'll go that way!

Yay! Swiper is giving everyone at the Eiffel Tower
their friendship bracelets! Oh, no! Fifi the skunk
is sneaking up on Swiper. Fifi will try to swipe the
bracelets. Help me stop Fifi! Say "Fifi, no swiping!"

Hooray! We stopped Fifi! Now all our friends
in France have friendship bracelets.
   There are many more bracelets to return.
¡Vámonos! Let's go!

We made it to Tanzania. This is my friend N'Dari. To say "hello" to N'Dari, we say "jambo." N'Dari says that everyone is waiting for the friendship bracelets at Mount Kilimanjaro.

Quick, we have to take a safari ride to the mountain!
Along the way we have to watch out for wild animals.
How many zebras, lions, giraffes, hippos, and elephants
do you see?

Hmm! I think I hear another wild animal. It sounds like a hyena. Do you see a hyena?

That's Sami the hyena! He's going to try to swipe the bracelets. Will you help me stop Sami? Say "Sami, no swiping!"

Yay! We stopped Sami! Come on, everyone! Come and get your friendship bracelets!

Now we have to bring the friendship bracelets to the Winter Palace in Russia. Do you see something that can fly us there? The hot-air balloon! Great idea!

We made it to Russia! But the Troll won't let us inside
the Winter Palace.

My friend Vladimir can help us. Vladimir says the Troll will open the gate if we make him laugh. Let's make silly faces to get the Troll to laugh! Make a silly face!
What great silly faces!

Our silly faces made the Troll laugh, and he opened the gate! And look! The Winter Palace is filled with lots of friends! Let's say "hello" to everyone. In Russian we say "preevyet!"

The children decorated the Winter Palace for Friendship Day! There are icicles, balloons, flags, snowmen, and even a dancing bear!

Fom-kah the bear is very sneaky. He's going to try to swipe the friendship bracelets. Help us stop Fomkah. Say "Fom-kah, no swiping!"

Yay! We stopped Fom-kah! Now we can return the friendship bracelets to our friends in Russia.

We have more bracelets to return. *¡Vámonos!*

We made it to the Great Wall of China. Wow! What a party! But we have to make sure these bracelets stay safe. Watch out for Ying Ying the weasel. If you see him, say "Ying Ying, no swiping!"

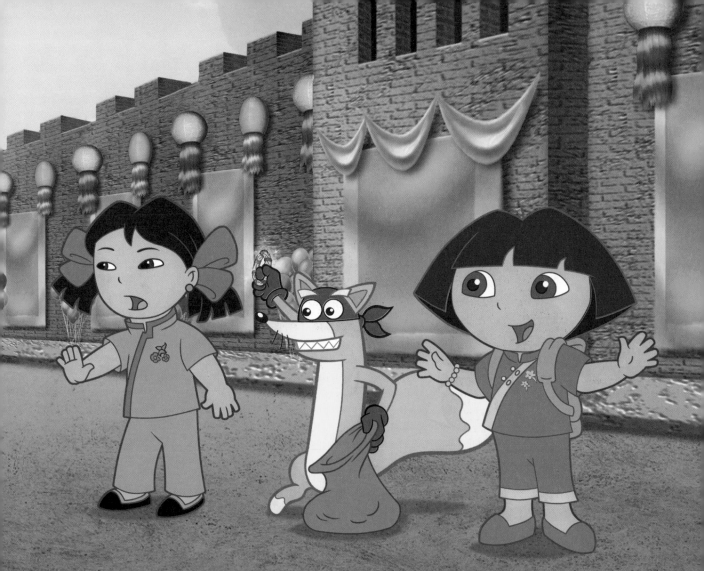

This is my friend Mei. To say "hello" to Mei, we say "knee-how." Mei is helping us give out the friendship bracelets.

Hooray! We returned all the friendship bracelets. Now we can start the Friendship Day celebration!

We made it back home for our Friendship Day celebration. We have eight friendship bracelets left. How many friends are at our party? *¡Siete!* Seven! They all get a friendship bracelet.

And there's one more bracelet! It's a friendship
bracelet for you—because you're such a great friend!

Wow! The bracelets are glowing! Rainbow sparkles are lighting the sky all over the world! Thanks for helping us save Friendship Day! Now we'll all be friends forever and ever! We did it!